LOCKED OUT

TAKING SIDES

LOCKED OUT

TAKING SIDES

PATRICK JONES

darbycreek
MINNEAPOLIS

Darby Creek
A division of Lerner Publishing Group, Inc.
241 First Avenue North
Minneapolis, MN 55401 USA

For reading levels and more information, look up this title at www.lernerbooks.com.

The images in this book are used with the permission of: © Juice Images/Alamy (young man); © iStockphoto.com/DaydreamsGirl (stone); © Maxriesgo/Dreamstime.com (prison wall); © Clearviewstock/Dreamstime.com, (prison cell).

Main body text set in Janson Text LT Std 12/17.5.
Typeface provided by Adobe Systems.

Library of Congress Cataloging-in-Publication Data

Jones, Patrick, 1961–
Taking sides / by Patrick Jones.
pages cm. — (Locked out)
Summary: At odds with his sister, Tina, fourteen, who says their father murdered their mother, Todd, fifteen, who claims it was self-defense, begins to lose faith in their father when he pressures Todd to get Tina to change her story, and being in separate foster homes only makes things harder.
ISBN 978-1-4677-5800-0 (lib. bdg. : alk. paper)
ISBN 978-1-4677-6184-0 (eBook)
[1. Brothers and sisters—Fiction. 2. Family violence—Fiction. 3. Fathers and sons—Fiction. 4. Foster home care—Fiction. 5. Minneapolis (Minn.)—Fiction.] I. Title.
PZ7.J7242Tak 2015
[Fic]—dc23 2014018200

Manufactured in the United States of America
1 – SB – 12/31/14

To Renee Reed, who takes the right side and
fights the good fight—P.J.

1

"It's my mother. He killed her."

Todd resisted the urge to rip the phone from his sister's hand. It was too late for that. He stayed where he was, kneeling on the blood-spattered kitchen floor, listening to Tina's teary side of the conversation with the 911 operator.

"Yes, my father," she said. Todd's hands tightened around the towel he held. He glared at his sister, but she was turned away from him, her ear pressed hard against the phone.

Then: "We're safe—he's gone. Send help, please."

A pause. Tina's breath, coming in rough half-sobs, was the only sound in the kitchen.

"My brother's here with me."

Another pause. *What could they be asking her?*

"He's—he's cleaning up the blood."

Another pause—another question?

"What about my dad?" Tina asked. Todd's father was gone. The thought scared him. Even more than the lifeless body of their mother, sprawled on the floor beside him.

"OK," Tina said shakily into the phone. She ended the call and wrapped her arms around her raised knees. "They're coming," she told Todd. "The police." She was shaking so hard she dropped her phone.

"You didn't have to make that call, Tina," Todd said quietly.

"She's lying on the floor *dead*, Todd!"

"The police can't change that," Todd shot back. No one could change what had just happened. The words that had sparked the fight. The knife in his mother's hand, pointed at her husband and children. His father's quick lunge and twist.

Todd felt sick to his stomach: the smell of the blood. "Look, we just need to stay calm. It's going to be OK."

Tina let out a wail. "Nothing is ever going to be OK again."

Todd didn't argue. He couldn't look at her, or at their mother's body. He had to focus. Closing his eyes, he turned his thoughts to his father: an innocent man on the run. *Dad, I'm with you. I'm on your side.*

2

Todd finished cleaning the blood from around his mother's prone body. His dad wouldn't like anyone to visit his house, even the police, and have it be such a mess. Tina was still curled up in a tiny ball in the corner. And crying, so much crying. Todd knew Dad wouldn't approve.

Todd carried the blood-soaked towel to the washer in the basement. Dumped in detergent. Turned the temperature to hot. He had a vague memory of his mom doing that in the past. This certainly wasn't the first time that his parents' arguments had left someone bloody. Once the cycle started, he returned to the kitchen, where Tina rocked back and forth like a baby.

Grabbing a garbage bag from the utility closet, he headed to the dining room. Started picking up the bits of broken china that littered the floor. It had been good china—his mom had been proud of it. She was proud of the whole house, of the airy rooms and the nice furniture and the carefully arranged knickknacks. Everything had always looked perfect, even on days when the cleaning lady didn't come.

Even on days when Todd's parents fought.

Many past fights had begun in this room, normally over something small. But this one had been something big.

Todd, Tina, get your stuff. You're moving in with me.

You walk out on us for a month, and now you think you can just show up and take the kids—

Well, you certainly can't take care of them, Katya. You've never known how to take care of them.

That's for the courts to decide.

Oh, you would know, after all the time you've been spending with those lady lawyers. Some corrupt judge doesn't get to tell me what to do when it comes to my family. You won't take my kids from me.

If it had just ended there, thought Todd. If Todd's mom had just let him and Tina pack some things and leave with their father. If she hadn't argued and threatened him. If Tina hadn't sided with their mom and refused to go. If their mom hadn't gone for the knife. Then none of this would've happened. There would've been no broken pieces for Todd to pick up, no blood to scrub away.

***

The police arrived before the ambulance. One of the cops checked Todd's mom for a pulse, then shook his head. He spoke into the radio on his shoulder, without any urgency. Todd didn't let himself look at the body. All he could think about was his father. Where was he? When would he be coming back?

The other cop, a big bruiser of a guy, came over to Todd. "I know this is hard, son, but can you tell me what happened?"

Todd paused. It had happened fast, but also in slow motion. Like football instant replay, which his dad hated. *The call is the call*, he'd say.

Never question a man's judgment.

Todd took a deep breath and got himself organized, like he'd do before a big test at school or before his turn in track or wrestling. (*Get yourself together, Junior, and you won't come apart under pressure.*) He glanced at his sister, still crying in the corner. She'd seen it too.

Tina lifted her head and wiped her nose with the sleeves of her Green River Academy blazer.

After one last deep breath, Todd spoke. "It was self-defense. My mother came—"

"No! No!" His sister's scream cut off his measured words.

The cop's eyes darted between Todd and Tina. "She had a knife," Todd said calmly.

Tina pulled herself from the floor, but stayed backed into the corner of the room. "Todd, that's not true. He hit her, like always, and then he stabbed her. Todd, why are—"

"My sister's wrong," Todd murmured. "It was self-defense."

The cop scratched his head like he was unsure what to say or do. He'd probably faced down stone cold killers and gang bangers. But he seemed stumped by these two kids who seemed to have everything—except one version of how their mother ended up dead. "The detectives are on their way. They'll sort this out."

"There's nothing to sort out," Todd said. "It was self-defense."

Tina shot to her feet and bolted across the room. Now she was standing in front of him, younger and shorter, but much louder. "Todd, why are you lying?"

3

Todd sat in the police interview room across from the detective: a forty-something guy, heavyset, freshly shaven. Pen in hand, notebook open on the table between them.

"Detective Murphy. Call me Steve if you like." Murphy flashed a smile, which Todd didn't return. He looked at his new Jordans and the tiny spots of blood that were ruining them.

Todd rarely watched crime shows on TV—his dad called it the idiot box—but he knew some things. "Do I need a lawyer?"

"You tell me, Todd," the detective said. "Did you do anything wrong?"

Todd paused again, wondering if wrong and

illegal were the same thing. "No, sir."

"That's good to know. So can you tell me what happened?"

"My parents were arguing," Todd began as he replayed the scene in his head. "Mom pulled a knife on him. Dad tried to take it away. They struggled and she got stabbed. If he hadn't done it, he'd have been the one dead, or one of us, instead of my mom."

As Murphy jotted down what Todd said, the door opened. Another officer, older, walked in and whispered something in Murphy's ear. Murphy didn't seem impressed. He turned back to Todd as the other officer left. "What were they fighting about?"

"About where we would live if they split up." He didn't offer any more details. Not the fact that his dad had already moved out of the house a month ago. Not the story of what life had been like before that, the years of his parents' fighting. (*Todd, a man's home is his castle. He's the king of everything, and everyone, in it.*)

"So is there a reason that you and your sister have such different versions of what happened?"

Murphy asked. He leaned across the table, notebook closed, palms open wide.

"She was in the corner crying," Todd said. "Her eyes were closed. I saw everything."

Detective Murphy asked more questions about the stabbing, Todd's parents, his relationship with his sister. To Todd, it seemed like they were running in circles.

"I need to get my things from my house," he said finally.

Murphy shot him an odd look: confused, hesitant. "Sorry, Todd, you can't go there now," he said. "It's a crime scene."

"But, I have to—"

"Todd, we really need to talk with your father. Where could we find him?"

"I don't know." He'd never been to his dad's new place. And even if he had, he wouldn't tell this cop about it.

"Do you know of any friends he might stay with?"

He shrugged.

"Family?"

"Nobody close."

"Todd, does your father have a girlfriend or —"

Todd kicked the table leg hard this time. "He's not like that. How dare you—"

"Calm down, Todd," Murphy said. "I didn't mean any offense. We just need to find him. Do you have your phone with you? Could you try calling him?"

Todd pulled out his phone. The call to his dad went right to voice mail. "He's not there."

Murphy motioned for the phone, but Todd buried it in his pocket as his dad's voice echoed in his mind again: *Todd, what happens in a man's home stays in his home. It's nobody's business.*

4

After another hour of questions, a bathroom break, and a fancy coffee they brought him, Detective Murphy finally told Todd he was done questioning him—"At this time."

"Can I go home now?" Todd asked. Murphy's big head swiveled on his thick neck.

"Wait here," he said, and left the room. As soon as Murphy was gone, Todd tried his father again, but without luck. He thought of calling his sister, but didn't. The police had taken them to the station in different cars, so he assumed she was talking to a detective too. *I hope this time she tells the truth*, he thought.

Todd waited in silence as a clock on the

wall ticked way too loudly. Another half hour went by. Then, finally, a sloppily dressed older man with uncombed grayish hair came into the room. He set a beat-up brown briefcase on the table and took a business card out of his pocket. "Todd, I'm Bob Hobson, a Hennepin County social worker."

Todd took the card Hobson held out, then crossed his arms. He didn't want to shake this guy's hand.

Hobson clicked open the briefcase and pulled out a legal pad with yellow paper. "So, the first thing we need to do is get you someplace to stay. Do have any relatives in Minneapolis?"

Todd shook his head. "My mom's from Russia. She doesn't have any family here. And my dad, well, he doesn't get along with his family. They live in Iowa, close to Des Moines. I don't remember where exactly. It doesn't matter. When can I go home?"

Hobson rubbed his eyes like they hurt. "Todd, how old are you?"

"I'm fifteen. My sister's fourteen."

"Well, that's too young for you to live on

your own. We'll take you to an emergency shelter for the night. I'll make some calls and see who has a free bed. Then tomorrow we'll work on long-term options."

"I just want to go home!" But even as Todd said the word "home" he felt uneasy. With his parents separated, it didn't feel like home anymore. His father coming and going, his mother hiding money and making whispering phone calls to lawyers. His home hadn't felt like one for a long time.

"I'm sorry Todd, that's not possible," Hobson said. "I know this is hard to process right now, but you need to look at the possibility that everything in your life is going to change very fast. You're probably not going to be back at your house for a long while. I'm not trying to make this any harder for you than it has to be. You've got to take things one day at a time . . ."

"Where's my sister?" Todd cut in. "Is she here? Is she coming with us to this shelter place?"

"I don't know what's going on with her," Hobson replied. "I was called about you. The police said since you're telling different stories, there should be no contact between you right now. Let's get going, OK?"

Todd didn't move. "I'd rather wait here until they find my father."

"Even if they do find him tonight, you won't be able to talk with him," Hobson explained. "He'll need to be booked, processed, arraigned, bail set. It might be a long time."

"How long is a long time?" Todd asked.

A sigh and another head shake was all he got in reply.

5

The lobby of the shelter was small, smelly, and dark. Todd imagined the entire place would be the same. He wanted to run.

Instead he stood as still as possible in the front hall while Hobson talked to a middle-aged man with too much beard and belly. Hobson laughed at something the man said. The noise felt to Todd like a slap in the face. The two men shook hands like old friends. They'd probably done this together a thousand times, like garbage men cleaning up other people's messes. After they spoke, Hobson left without saying good-bye to Todd.

"Sit down, Todd," the guy said as he locked

the door behind Hobson. He had a huge jangly key ring like a dungeon master in a video game.

Trained by his father to follow orders, Todd did as he was told.

"I'm Brenden Jackson, night manager and . . ." His mouth kept moving, but Todd wasn't listening to a word of it. The rush of the evening had crashed down hard, and his thoughts were getting fuzzy with exhaustion. "Todd, are you listening?"

Todd nodded as he fought to stay awake.

"What school do you attend?" Jackson asked. Like Hobson, he was writing everything down, which seemed stupid to Todd. He wouldn't be here long enough for any of this to matter. His dad would clear up the confusion, his sister would tell the truth, and life would be normal again.

"Todd? Your school?"

"Green River Academy in Minnetonka."

Jackson frowned. "That's a long way from here. It may be tough tomorrow to arrange transport—"

Todd cut him off. "I don't want to go to school tomorrow."

"You have to go to school."

Todd finally made eye contact. He pulled in his breath, pushed out his chest. "My mom's dead. My dad's missing. My sister's someplace else. I'm not ready for school with all that."

Jackson started to disagree, but Todd wasn't having any of it. *If you let people bully you once*, his father had said, *they'll bully you twice. Stand up for yourself. Be a man.*

Todd stood up and walked toward the door. "I'm going home—"

"You can't leave." Todd pulled on the locked door. Jackson didn't move. "Sit down, Todd."

Todd pulled harder on the door and then pounded on it until his hands bled.

The evening had started with blood. It would end with it too.

6

"We'll be in touch, Todd," Detective Murphy said after another few hours of questioning at the station. Todd had stayed in bed at the shelter all day. He'd refused to go to school, eat, or do anything until Murphy picked him up. Deep down, Todd couldn't say no to a police officer.

"Where's my sister?" Todd asked once again.

"I'm sorry, Todd, but I can't talk to you about that," said Murphy. "Someone from the County will be by to pick you up in a few minutes. Then you'll be able to run by your house and get a few things, but it's still a crime scene until we . . ." Murphy stopped in mid-sentence like he had a secret to keep. Todd wondered if

Murphy was purposely making him feel like *he* was the criminal.

"Well, anyway, I'll walk you to the lobby." Murphy led Todd from the small room with hard chairs to a larger room with harder chairs.

"You Todd Morgan?" a middle-aged African American woman asked. Her colorful dress stood out against the drabness of the lobby. "I'm Mikayla Franklin, Hennepin County Social Services."

Todd nodded and accepted another business card thrust in his hand. "This way, Todd." Todd followed as Franklin talked. He was going home, but the bad dream seemed far from over.

***

The police were still at the house when Todd and Franklin arrived. Everything looked the same. "We're still working on finding a long-term placement for you," Franklin said. She talked fast—*In a hurry to get rid of me*, Todd thought. "So just pack enough for two nights and school tomorrow."

On the way to his room, he peeked into his sister's room. Her book bag, which was always on the floor next to her dresser, was gone, so she'd already been home and left.

"Hurry up!" Franklin called from the living room.

Todd slowly walked into his room. He gathered up his book bag and charger. Packed his gym bag for his wrestling meet. Folded a day's worth of clothes into another small bag.

"All set?" Franklin said when Todd returned to the living room.

"No, I need one more thing." Todd headed for the wall full of photos and awards. He snatched the photo of him and his dad, with Todd's division wrestling championship trophy between them. Gently, he placed the photo inside the small bag. Then Franklin hurried him toward the door. Todd closed it and started to lock it.

"Leave the key with me," Franklin said. "The police may need it to process more of the scene later."

"I'm not giving my key to strangers,"

Todd said.

"Todd, we're talking about the police." Todd said nothing. Franklin sighed. "Let me give you a realistic preview of what your life is going to be like in the short term until this all gets sorted out. You are going to meet a whole of lot of people you don't know, like me, like lawyers, and cops, and foster parents. You can either trust that we're looking out for you, or you can keep that attitude and make it harder for everyone—mostly yourself and your sister. Is that really what you want?"

Todd handed the key to Franklin and slammed the door behind him.

He didn't say anything about the spare key his mom kept under the garden edging. Unless Tina got to it first, it would be waiting for him when he came home again.

***

"Mr. Parker, thanks for working with us on such short notice," Franklin said. Todd stood with her outside a large run-down house in northeast Minneapolis. "This is Todd Morgan."

"Where does he go to school?" asked Parker, a large man with a small voice.

"Green River Academy." Todd and Franklin answered at the same time.

"Does he drive?" Parker asked. Todd shook his head. He'd planned to take driver's ed this summer.

"Well, then he's not going to Green River unless he has a limo take him," Parker said. "So it looks like he's got the day off tomorrow. Try to get him by noon so I can get on with my day."

"By law you have to provide him—" Franklin started

"Not to a private school I don't," Parker cut in. "Check the rules."

"Then you need to get him enrolled at Northeast," Franklin said. Todd didn't know much about Northeast, except it seemed every time there was a gang shooting on the news, it involved a kid who'd dropped out of that school.

Parker mumbled something Todd couldn't hear, which was fine. He wasn't interested in anything Parker or Franklin had to say.

"OK, Todd, I'll see you later." Franklin

smiled, but Todd could tell she was faking, just like Murphy. Just like his sister. Everybody lied to him but his dad. Franklin turned and walked briskly toward her car.

"All right, get inside," sighed Parker.

Todd kicked his bloody shoe against the creaky wooden front porch, then followed the man. The inside of the house was dimly lit, but Todd could see it was cluttered, disorganized. Nearby but out of sight, he heard stomping feet and raised voices—boys arguing.

Exhaustion settled into his bones. "Where's my room?" he asked.

"Room? This is an emergency foster placement, not a Hyatt. Your room is there." Parker pointed at a sofa in the front room. On it was a small pillow and thin blanket. "Breakfast is at 6:30. If you're up, you eat. If you're not, you don't. Anything else you want to ask?"

Yeah, Todd thought, *a lot of things. Where's Tina? Why are the police blaming my dad for what happened? How did our lives fall apart so fast?*

But by now he knew better than to expect answers.

7

Todd's phone jolted him awake. He fished it from his pocket. It was a text from Benton, one of his wrestling pals at Green River. Before he read it, Todd paused and soaked in the strange surroundings. From another room, he heard loud voices, lots of them—kids' voices. He wasn't at home—he was somewhere else—his father was missing—his mother was dead—his sister was—where? Why?

It's all over the news, said Benton's text.

Todd didn't need to ask what "it" meant. *Do they know where my dad is?* he texted back.

No, they're looking for him, Benton responded. Then he followed up with a bunch more questions, one per text, ending with *How's Tina?*

Todd knew Benton, like lots of his friends, had a thing for his sister. Todd scrolled through the string of questions, trying to decide if he could answer any of them.

A meaty hand swiped the phone out of Todd's. "No phones before school," said Parker as he put Todd's cell in his pocket. "Get cleaned up." He pointed toward the hall.

"I'm hungry," Todd said.

Parker pulled out Todd's phone and showed him the time. 7:00. "I warned you."

Two black boys, about ten or eleven years old, ran out of the kitchen and past the couch. One pointed at Todd's face, and both snickered. Todd wanted to ask, "What's so funny?" but the kids had already dashed into another room. He stood up, keeping the thin blanket around him, and headed into the bathroom.

When he turned on the light and stared in the mirror at his face, he saw why the boys had been laughing. During the night while he slept, someone had taken a black marker and written the word "cracker" on his forehead.

With no phone or computer access in the Parker house, Todd sat watching TV, mostly local news. As Benton had said, the story was everywhere. They kept showing the same picture of his parents, from some fundraiser they'd attended. They looked so happy. Todd didn't know what had changed. Maybe money. A lot of the fights had been about money. Money being spent, money mysteriously disappearing . . . most of the details had been fuzzy to Todd.

The doorbell rang. "Todd, get your stuff!" Parker yelled from the other room. "That's someone from the County to pick you up." Todd thought the way everyone said "the County" made it sound like the Empire in the Star Wars movies.

Todd gathered his few things while Parker opened the door and whispered back and forth to a young man, maybe thirty, black, well dressed. Then the young man came over to Todd, hand outstretched. "Todd, Bill Martin, HC Human Services."

Todd shook his hand. A light grip, not firm

like Todd's father had taught him. "What's going on?" Todd asked.

Martin talked way too fast, yet repeated himself. He also threw around lots of initials: PSF, APB, HCMC. But the main point was that Todd was headed to a new foster home. Martin used the words "excellent placement" about five times.

"He took my phone," Todd said, pointing toward Parker. Parker heaved a sigh, then took the phone from his pocket.

Todd reclaimed his phone, picked up his bags, and headed for the door. On the porch, Todd told Martin, "I have a wrestling meet today, at four. The bus leaves Green River at—"

"Sorry, Todd," Martin said. "That won't be possible, at least not today."

"Can I at least go back to school tomorrow?" Todd asked as he climbed into the backseat of the car. These cramped compacts were a far cry from the Lexus sedans that his father traded in for a newer model every year or two. "I can't afford to miss another day. I don't want to get behind and—"

Martin cut him off again. He seemed to like talking more than listening. "Todd, the law requires us to keep you in your same school, but only for public schools. The County can provide you with a bus pass to get to Green River, or you can attend Northeast High just down the street. Of course, even that might only be temporary."

"What do you mean temporary?" Todd asked. He felt like a tennis ball on the Green River court.

"This is a short-term placement, thirty days," Martin explained. "After that we'll have to set you up with something else. With your father probably going to prison—"

"He's not going to prison!" Todd burst out. "He's innocent."

Martin sighed, "OK," but he didn't sound as if he believed Todd—more like he just wasn't willing to discuss it. He turned on the radio, and a few seconds later he answered a phone call.

Martin had been jabbering into his cell for a solid five minutes when Todd's own phone rang.

Todd didn't recognize the number, so he let it go, but the same number kept calling. Martin, absorbed in his own phone call, didn't seem to notice.

Finally, when the radio was in the middle of an especially loud song, Todd picked up and whispered into the phone, "Who is this?"

8

“Can you talk?” The voice on the other end was Todd’s father.

Todd lowered the phone. “Can we pull over?” Todd called to Martin over the music. “I need to use the bathroom.”

“Can’t it wait? I’m on a tight schedule.”

“If I piss all over your car, what’s that going to do your schedule?” Todd snapped. Hearing his dad’s voice had energized him, making him feel like a man.

Martin sighed and pulled into a Taco Bell parking lot. Todd almost didn’t wait for the car to stop before opening the door. “Hey, get me a coffee. Get a receipt,” Martin said and handed Todd a five dollar bill.

After slamming the car door as hard as he could, Todd walked into the restaurant. Once safely inside the building, he spoke into the phone, hand over the receiver. "Dad, are you OK?"

"I'm fine, Junior," his father replied. "Look, this is a pre-pay cell and I don't have much time left on it. I've been talking to people, lawyers. This is all very complicated."

"What do you want me to do?" Todd asked.

There was a pause. Behind Todd, people placed orders at the counter like it was just another day.

"Dad, are you there? What do you want me to do?"

"Have you spoken with Tina since your mom came at me?"

"No." Todd started to explain all the things he'd gone through, but his dad cut him off.

"You have to talk to your sister," his dad said in a tone as strong as his handshake. "I think she's got the wrong idea about things. You saw what happened, right? How your mother came after me with a knife and how, to save my life, and yours and Tina's, I had to fight back."

The instant replay ran again in Todd's head, but it seemed fuzzier than before. "Yes."

"And that's the story you've told the police, right?"

"Yes, sir."

"So you need to talk to Tina, to make sure she says the same thing."

"Yes, sir."

"I'm staying with a friend, but I know I have to turn myself in. That's what my lawyer says, but I don't want to do that until I know that Tina's on board. It's up to you, Junior."

"I won't let you down, sir."

"I know you won't." The words were so clear and strong, it almost seemed to Todd like his father was standing right beside him, hand on his shoulder.

"I'll call back in a few hours, but you can't tell anyone we've talked, got it?"

"Yes, sir."

"You're a good son." The line went dead.

***

"What took you so long?" asked Martin when Todd got back to the car and handed him his stupid coffee. "And where's my receipt?"

Todd felt the slip of paper and the change in his pocket, along with his growing collection of social workers' business cards. "Where's my sister?"

"I can't talk about that, Todd."

"Why not?" Todd asked. "She's my only family. She needs me! Why can't I see her?"

"Not my call. Detective Murphy said no contact."

The conversation was clearly over, but Todd's head pounded with words he was holding back: *Why does he get to control my life?* Even in his own mind, Todd wasn't sure whether *he* was Murphy, Martin, or . . .

He shoved the thought away and slumped in the backseat.

9

A large white van filled the small driveway of the house. Smaller than the Parker place, this house didn't seem as run down, although Todd wasn't holding out much hope for the inside.

At the door, an older man greeted them. Martin introduced him as Mr. Sorensen. He wore a yellow polo shirt and a green sweater. Todd noticed he moved slowly and spoke even slower. Martin and Todd stepped into the house, which smelled like the wrestling room after a hard practice.

"Mr. Morgan, put your things in box five."

Mr. Morgan sounds so weird, Todd thought. *That's my dad, not me.*

The older man pointed toward a row of numbered cardboard boxes. Todd's name, written on a piece of masking tape, was on box five. As he put his bags in the box, Todd saw tiny remnants of other pieces of tape, fragments of names. He was hit by a deep longing for his own house, with his own stuff, where he wasn't just borrowing space for the short term.

"There's coffee in the kitchen if you want it, one cup a day," the man said. "Or if you want a soda, you can have that instead. One of those a day. If you want another, it's a dollar."

"How long am I going to be here?" Todd asked.

"That's up to you, Mr. Morgan," Sorensen said.

"If it is, then I'm leaving now." Todd started to lift his bags from the dumpy brown box.

"And where would you go?" Martin asked. "I'm sorry, but until things get sorted out, you're in the system now and this is the placement. An excellent placement, I might add."

Sorensen reached out his hand, but not for a handshake. In his right hand, he held a bunch of papers that looked like the small booklet coaches handed out at the start of the season. "This is my house. These are my rules."

Todd took the papers.

"You violate any of these rules, I call the county and you end up elsewhere."

Todd glanced at the front page. Under the headline Sorensen House Rules was: "*Watch ye therefore: for ye know not when the master of the house cometh. Mark 13:35.*" Each page, Todd noticed, had a similar Bible quote at the top. There were twenty pages of rules and quotes.

"If I'm going to be here for a while, I need to get more things from my house," Todd said. He wondered if asking for things was against the rules or if it would cost him a dollar.

Martin sighed and looked at his watch, his normal routine. "OK, last trip. I'm a social worker, not a transportation system. Speaking of which, here's your bus pass."

Todd took the small card and tucked it in his pocket. He'd never had a bus pass before. "Good, I'll use it to go to Green River."

Martin sighed, then looked at his watch. "That's your choice. I hope you like sitting on the bus and don't like sleeping. That'll take two hours, I bet."

10

Martin was wrong. It took more than two hours to get from North Minneapolis to the west suburbs by bus. And Todd had been standing in the wrong place to catch the bus from downtown, which added to his time. He'd never been late to school before. In a way, it felt like this was his first day at Green River, back in the Lower School. Like all the years he'd spent there counted for nothing now.

The guard at the door stopped him and directed him toward the main office. Another first. His dad had long ago made it clear that winding up in the principal's office was unacceptable.

At the main desk, Todd said, "I'm late. What happens?"

The office manager stared at him, looked over her shoulder at a coworker, and then dialed her phone. "Wait just a moment," she told Todd before speaking into the phone, almost secretively: "Todd Morgan's here."

A moment later she hung up the phone. "Dr. Marsh wants to see you, Todd. She'll be back in just a minute. You can wait in her office." She pointed Todd in the right direction. Todd did as he was told.

The office was nothing like he'd expected. It was warm, filled with photos, awards, banners, all of it celebrating Green River. Todd sat in a comfy tan chair across from Dr. Marsh's empty desk. Checked his phone. His dad hadn't called back yet. No one else had called or texted except for Benton yesterday morning.

"Todd, thank you for waiting." Dr. Marsh strode into the office. She wasn't alone. Standing with her were Coach Colter and Mrs. Lang, the school counselor he was assigned to but never visited. "Everyone in the Green River family was shocked and very saddened by the news about your mother. We're so sorry for your loss. Your mom was a lovely woman."

Of all the words Todd had heard from people on the other side of desks in the past few days, the single word *was* felt like a blow to the gut. His mom belonged to the past tense.

"Is there anything we can do?" Dr. Marsh asked. Todd didn't know what to say. It was like asking a starving man what he'd like to eat. There were too many needs to make one choice.

"My dad's innocent," Todd blurted out. It was the only thought he could wrap his head around. "It was self-defense. I was there. I saw the whole thing. He'll get his name cleared soon. Then things will go back to normal."

The adults exchanged glances. Todd was so sick of adults doing that. Doubting him. Not listening to him.

Todd decided to change the subject. "Coach, I'm sorry I missed the meet yesterday. I couldn't call. Everything was happening so fast and—"

"Don't worry about that right now, Todd,"

said Coach Colter. He had an odd look on his face. Embarrassed, almost.

"So I'm still on the team? Even though I no-showed?"

"Well . . . uh . . ." Todd could tell that wasn't a yes.

Coach Colter looked at Dr. Marsh, who finally spoke. "These are very unique circumstances, Todd. Do you intend to continue at Green River Academy?"

Todd didn't like the tone. It sounded to him like the answer she wanted was no. "Of course. I mean, I know I'm late today, but that was just because the bus was running behind schedule."

"We're not even sure who to talk to about this," said Dr. Marsh carefully. "Who are you living with?"

Todd explained the Sorensen placement in as few words as possible.

"OK," said Dr. Marsh. "We'll need to do some following up. I can't promise anything until I know more."

"What do you mean?" asked Todd. "You don't need to promise anything. I've already said I'll take the bus here every day. I won't be late again . . ."

"Todd, we just wonder if—with everything happening—if Green River is the best place for you."

"What do you mean? Of course it is. All my friends are here. And my whole family's gone here—my dad went here."

"Yes, and that's why we've allowed you to continue without interruption this year, even though your father—" Dr. Marsh stopped speaking suddenly.

"What about my father?"

"He hasn't paid your tuition yet for the year," Marsh said, sounding embarrassed, even though Todd felt the humiliation was all his. "I thought you knew."

The adults continued talking about what was best for Todd, as though he wasn't sitting in front of them. As he listened, it suddenly hit him. When Dr. Marsh had asked if Green River was "still the best place" for Todd, what she'd really wanted to know was whether Todd could afford Green River's high tuition. That was what they were really worried about. He felt his face grow hot.

Todd reached down for the gym bag that held his wrestling gear and tossed it at Coach Colter's feet. "Can I go now?" he asked.

Dr. Marsh nodded, a tiny gesture, almost like she didn't want the other adults to see it. *They don't want me here*, Todd thought. *Some Green River family.*

Todd left the office and took off toward his locker. The bell rang for the end of first period and suddenly the hallways were swarming with people—students, teachers, staff. It seemed like everyone was either deliberately not looking at him, or staring at him. He saw two girls point, whisper, and laugh. As if anything was funny about what was happening to him. Suddenly, he switched direction and headed toward the ninth grade section. Like a cop on a stakeout, he planted himself next to Tina's locker.

As Todd half-expected, Tina didn't show up. Then he spotted Tina's best friend Ashley down the hallway, in the center of a group of girls. With a burst of speed, Todd cut into the group. "Ash, where's Tina?"

11

The bus ride from Green River back downtown and then south to Southeast High School seemed to take forever, maybe because Todd had so much on his mind. He wasn't sure about going back to Green River, but he was positive he needed to see his sister. Ash hadn't given up Tina's new school, so Todd had gotten the info from one of her other friends who had a crush on him.

Unlike Northeast High, which he had no intention of attending, Todd had been to Southeast for sports events. He'd won his first wrestling match as a freshman at a Southeast meet. Although most of his buddies played basketball as their winter sport, Todd's dad pushed him toward wrestling, as well as cross country and track. (*Even if your team loses, you can still win. You don't need to rely on anyone but yourself. That's a good life lesson, Junior.*)

Todd knew he couldn't get into the school, so he waited across the street. He texted Benton and other wrestling buddies, asking how the meet had gone, but no one texted back.

An hour later, high-schoolers were pouring out the front doors. Todd immediately called his sister's phone.

The call went to voicemail. Todd wanted to leave another message, but Tina's mailbox was full. Had she listened to any of his messages begging her to talk to him? Why wasn't she returning his calls? Was it her choice, or were the police not allowing her to call?

And then he saw Tina emerging from the front door, alone, her head down. He'd have his answers soon.

Pushing his way through the crowd, he shouted her name. Tina stopped, stared at Todd for a second, and then started running. Even though she dropped her book bag to gain speed, Todd was faster. He caught her by the curb and grabbed her arms. "Tina, why are you running from me? Why won't you answer my calls?"

Tina refused to look at him until he forced her chin up. She was crying. Todd wondered how many times she had cried during the last week. Had she ever stopped? "Tina, you have to listen to me."

He placed a hand on her shoulder, just like his dad used to do. "I'm not sure what you think you saw, but you've got it all wrong. Mom came at Dad. He was defending himself, protecting us too. You've got to tell the police the truth. You—"

"Todd, leave me alone!" Tina shouted. "I can't talk to you. I won't talk to you!"

"Tina, listen, you've got to do the right thing here, for me, for you, for Dad. If you—"

"He killed her, Todd!" Tina started to shout more, but tears choked out her words.

Todd's clasped both his sister's shoulders, just as his coach would do before a match. He needed to get her focused, to get her to listen to him, to their dad. "Listen, Tina, it wasn't his fault! Anyway, nothing we do or say now can bring her back. But we *can* bring Dad back."

"You think I want him back?" Tina screamed.

"He's our family! That's what matters—"

"What matters," Tina shrieked at the top of her lungs, "is our dead mother!"

Todd could ignore Tina's words, but not her tears, falling fast. He loosened his grip on her. "Todd, why aren't you upset?" she demanded. "Why are—"

Todd cut her off. "She's gone, Tina. Dad's still alive. He's the one that we—"

Tina tore herself away from her brother. Todd stood frozen for a moment, long enough for Tina to scoop up her book bag and head back toward the school. "Tina, wait! Just wait—"

It only took him a second to overtake her again. He spun her around—she was sobbing so hard her whole body shook.

A deep male voice yelled, "Hey! Let her go!" Some teacher guy was running toward them.

"What's going on here?"

"She's my sister . . ."

"No!" shouted Tina, pushing him away again. "Get away from me."

"Tina, what are you—"

"Get away!" she yelled as the teacher guy stepped between them. "Just stay away!"

"No, listen," Todd said desperately, speaking to the teacher now. "She's my sister, I just want to talk to her for a minute."

"I'm not!" Tina shrieked from behind the teacher. "He's not family!"

"Look, I can prove it!" Todd pulled out his phone and pulled up a photo of the two of them together—a selfie he'd taken a few weeks before, just after a wrestling meet she'd come to with her friends. "See, there we are together—"

In a tear-choked voice, Tina talked over him. "He's my ex-boyfriend, OK? He's been stalking me. Please, can you just call the police?"

Todd gaped at her. How could she be so afraid of him that she would say something like this? "Tina—!"

The teacher was already ushering her back toward the building. "Come on, let's get you inside first," the guy said in a low voice Todd wasn't meant to hear. As soon as they got back into the school, the teacher would probably do exactly what Tina had asked—call the police.

"It's not true!" Todd shouted after them. "She's lying! I'm telling the truth!" Then he swore under his breath and took off running.

12

It was the call he'd been dreading. Unknown caller. His father. Todd didn't want to answer, but knew he had to, if only to hear his dad's voice again. He picked up and struggled to hear through the chatter of the other bus riders and their screaming children. Out of the corner of his eye, Todd saw two young kids, a brother and sister, at their mom's feet. The mom had a phone pressed to one ear, and covered her other ear to block out the sounds of her kids.

"Junior, it's Dad. Have you seen Tina?"

"Yes, sir."

"And?"

Todd paused and thought for a second about

hanging up, jumping off the bus at the next stop, and running. With his cross country endurance, Todd knew he could run a long, long time.

"Junior, are you there?" His father said. "Answer me."

Todd imagined the hard look on his dad's face when he told him he'd failed. He'd seen it so many times that it was burned on his brain. Jaw set tight, dark eyes flat. It was the look that said, "Todd, I'm not mad at you, just disappointed."

"I saw her," Todd confessed.

"And?"

Todd told his father about his talk with Tina, including Tina denying that she knew him.

"You see what I mean, Junior," Dad says. "She lies. You tell that story to the police."

"Why should I talk to the police again?"

"I'm coming in. My lawyer told me that if you couldn't make your sister understand the truth, I'd have to surrender. Since you couldn't do what I asked, I have no choice."

"I'm sorry I let you down," Todd choked out. He tried to imagine the look on his father's face. Was it still the scowl of disappointment? Or was there a glimmer of understanding? Of acceptance? Todd wanted to join the children crying at their mother's feet on the bus. "Dad, what's going to happen?"

"I'll get booked at the county jail, arraigned, and then post bond. I'll be out by morning."

"Can I see you?"

Todd's father didn't answer. It sounded like he had his hand over the phone and was having another conversation. Who was he talking to? Where was he? But even as Todd asked himself these questions, another one emerged: *Why doesn't he ask about me?* His father hadn't asked how he was doing, where he was living, anything.

"My lawyer says it's complicated, but he understands the system better than I do."

The System. Just like "the County," but bigger.

The bus pulled into the downtown bus mall where he'd transfer to the next bus, to take him to the next transfer, and then to Sorensen's place.

"I'll try to talk to Tina again, if that's what you want," Todd said as people pushed past him.

More muffled conversations. Todd followed the mom and her crying children off the bus. "Don't. My lawyer says you might get me into trouble for witness tampering. Might make it worse."

"Witness tampering?"

"My lawyer found out that Tina's talking to the police. I mean lying to them," Dad said."If it goes to trial, your sister is going to testify against me."

With that, the line went dead. Todd paused on the sidewalk. Stared at the phone. His dad had hung up on him. Given up on him.

Well, I'm not giving up yet. Todd opened the map feature on his phone and pulled up directions to the county jail.

13

Todd shivered in the cold outside the Sorensen house. Just as the rule book said, if a resident wasn't in by curfew, he'd find the door locked. Todd had waited all night for his father to show up at the jail, but he never did. When Todd had gone inside to inquire, the jail staff had been no help. Tired and discouraged, Todd had taken another long bus ride, only to find himself locked out.

When the door opened the next morning for the other foster kids to leave for school, Todd raced inside. "I'm giving you a one-time pass since you seem like a good kid," Sorensen said. "It happens again, you're out."

Todd nodded. He didn't want to waste a single word, an ounce of energy on Sorensen or the other soul-crushing cogs in The System. He ducked into the kitchen, grabbed a cola from the fridge, and gulped it down. Then he went to the room he shared with a city kid named Antonio. It was a mess—like there had been a party there without him.

Todd grabbed clean clothes, took a quick shower, and raced back to the kitchen. Still tired, he filled a Styrofoam cup with the sludge that Sorensen called coffee. Still, it was warm caffeine. He drained the cup, then filled it again.

"That's a dollar," Sorensen said.

Todd pulled out his wallet. It was empty. "I'll pay you later."

"Price goes up later."

Todd recalled seeing an ATM near the downtown bus stop. He'd be tardy for school anyway, so what difference did another ten minutes make? What difference did anything make?

"Make sure you check out the chore wheel," Sorensen said as Todd bounded out the door. *I hate this,* Todd thought. The chore wheel, the caffeine cost, Sorensen, his house, his rules, all of it.

On the bus, he tried playing games on his phone, but it was too noisy, and he was too distracted. He found the app for the local newspaper, downloaded it, and saw the story. His father had surrendered to police early in the morning and was being held in the Public Safety Facility, some fancy name for the jail, pending his arraignment and bond hearing.

When the bus finally reached downtown, Todd raced to the ATM. His dad had set up an account for him and put in twenty dollars each week. If Todd didn't spend the entire twenty, his dad would give him more next week, so he'd built a cash reserve. Lately, as his parents fought more, his dad put extra money in. Todd pushed in his card, typed the code, and hit the button to withdraw twenty. The screen flashed "insufficient funds." He took out the card, started over, and got the same result. He started to try it a third time when he heard a man's irritated voice behind him. "Kid, I've got places to go. Let's move."

Todd put the card back in his wallet and raced toward his next bus, but he arrived just in time to see it leaving. The next one was in twenty minutes. Hating to waste time, he hustled back to the jail, went inside and waited in a long line to speak to the person at the desk. "I want to know when I can visit my—"

The uniformed man pointed at a sign which showed visiting hours: Monday 6 to 10 p.m., and Wednesday, Friday, and Saturday 8 to 10 a.m. Today was Thursday. "How do I visit?"

The answer this time was a sheet of paper and another set of rules. *At least there are no Bible verses*, he thought. Todd started to ask another question, but the guard looked past him and yelled "next." Todd knew that look pretty well by now. A lot of people had turned out to be pretty good at acting like he didn't exist. He stepped out of line and glanced at the sheet that read "Visitors under 18 must be accompanied by a parent or legal guardian." *If my dad's in jail and my mom's dead*, Todd thought, *who is my guardian?*

14

When Todd arrived at the school, he went directly to Dr. Marsh's office.

"Todd!" Dr. Marsh looked surprised to see him. Maybe even a little nervous? But no, he was imagining that. Dr. Marsh wouldn't be frightened of him, would she? "Come in. Have a seat. What can I do for you?"

"Did you do your following up?" Todd asked, borrowing the phrase she'd used the day before. "Do you know who my legal guardian is? Is it Sorensen?"

For all her degrees, Dr. Marsh seemed puzzled by the question. "I'm still not sure. I haven't had a chance to look into your situation more closely . . ."

Todd reached into his wallet. He pulled out the business cards of all the social workers he'd come in contact with the past week. He placed them on the table like he was dealing poker. "Or maybe it's one of these people. I need to find out so I can visit my dad."

Dr. Marsh studied him for a few seconds. "Do you think that's a good idea?" she said. "I mean given the circumstances."

Why does she use that word so much? Todd asked himself. "He's innocent," Todd snapped, for what seemed like the millionth time.

Dr. Marsh's shoulders tensed. The way his mom's used to, when she was expecting a blow. "I'll see what I can find out, Todd," she said. "About your legal status. But for now, maybe it's best if you go to class and just try to get through the day."

Dr. Marsh seems to care, Todd thought. *But that's her job.* None of these people really cared about him. And he couldn't visit the only person who did care. He slammed the door when he left Dr. Marsh's office, and then the door to the office suite. Todd wanted to walk down more halls, find more doors, and slam them all.

He couldn't wait to get to his locker, if only to slam it shut. As he got close, he saw something taped to it. It was a sympathy card, signed by the wrestling team. Some standard lines about being "sorry for your loss." Still, he had to hold back tears as he read it.

Then he felt a tap on his back. "Todd—sorry, man." It was Benton. Benton, who hadn't returned any of his calls or texts.

"Thanks, Bent." Todd had only so much anger left and didn't want to waste it on Benton.

"Man, we've got the out-of-town tournament this weekend, or we'd be there for you."

"Be where?"

"At your mom's funeral."

"When is it?" Todd asked. No one had told him. How could that be?

Benton blinked a couple times—no other sign of surprise. Benton was tough to rattle. Once, Todd would've said the same about himself. "Saturday morning at ten, but like I said, we'll be out of town. Sorry, man."

Todd nodded, opened the locker, took out

nothing, and slammed the door. The jolt of it shot through his system like he'd been taken down in a match.

"Bent, can I ask you something?"

"Sure, man."

"Can I borrow a dollar?"

15

Todd hadn't expected so many people to show up at the jail on a Friday morning, but the line stretched out the door. Noisy, crowded, and full of screaming children. If this adult, something called a guardian ad litem, didn't show, he'd start screaming too.

After getting home from Green River yesterday, he'd asked Sorensen who his legal guardian was. Sorensen was as unhelpful as ever. So Todd had called every number on the cards he'd been given, but only Martin, the guy who dumped him with Sorensen, bothered to return his call. It was like the adults were playing a game of musical chairs, and the music stopped on Martin.

Martin explained that pending the outcome of his father's case, a judge had given the county temporary custody of Todd. Sorensen was his acting legal guardian in most matters, but a guardian ad litem—Mrs. Peters—would advocate for Todd. Todd hated to beg, but he'd come close when he got in touch with the Peters lady. And she'd agreed to meet him at the jail this morning.

So where was she? Even though the sign said "no cell phone while in line," Todd took out his phone and started to dial the number he'd been given. Nothing happened. The phone had power, but it was frozen. He turned it off and on again hoping for a different result. Nothing.

"Todd?" A skinny woman with long straight black hair was coming toward him.

"My phone isn't working," was his greeting in return.

"That's all right. I'm Peggy Peters. Let's have a seat."

"I don't want to lose my place in line."

"I know, but there's a lot of paperwork to do first," Peters said. "To be honest, you might not be able to visit him today. I've made a few calls, but the system is complicated."

"When does he get out?" Todd had read up on bail. As soon as his dad posted bond, he'd be set free until his trial.

"Your father's attorney hasn't spoken with you?" asked Peters.

"No."

"Your father might be in jail a long time," she said gently. "He couldn't make bail."

Todd swallowed back the urge to throw something breakable. Why wasn't he being informed? Why wasn't he allowed to go to hearings or get this information first hand? He hated having to trust other people. "Why not?"

"I don't know. But I'm your advocate, so we'll figure it out together." She handed him some papers and slowly went through them, eating up valuable time. *Yet another set of rules. Just great.*

"This explains what I can and can't do for you. Remember, I'm a representative on your behalf, but you are your own best advocate. It's up to you to communicate your needs."

"I need to see my dad!" Todd shouted. It didn't matter if his dad was angry, disappointed, or both. All that mattered was seeing him. "No more excuses!" He wasn't the only one shouting. Family members were shouting at family members, and guards were shouting at everyone. The lobby was louder than a pep rally.

"I understand that, Todd. I'll do what I can."

Todd and Peters got back in line. Moments later, an older man with a cane joined the line, but the guard told him to leave. "No passes issued in the last fifteen minutes."

The old man cursed under his breath and made his way slowly out the door. Just as slowly, Todd and Peters advanced in the line. Todd started to empty his pockets.

"Driver's license," the guard said. Peters handed hers over. Todd stood frozen.

"I don't have one," he mumbled. "I have my school ID."

"I need a valid state or federally issued photo ID. If a person does not have such an ID, they can apply for one at..." The guard rattled off his speech like he'd given it a million times.

"A school ID is not a valid ID for admission to the visiting area."

Peters started to argue with the guard, but Todd could tell he wasn't listening. Like so many times over the past few days, another set of adults he barely knew argued about what was best for Todd. Todd didn't even have the energy to be angry. In fact, the tension in his muscles was easing. As if he'd been working himself up for a wrestling match he knew he'd lose, only to find out it was canceled. He tried to get some of the rage back—some of the strength he'd felt a few minutes ago when he demanded to see his father. But all he could feel was a strange, hollow relief.

Maybe it was for the best after all. Maybe he wasn't ready yet to see his father face to face—and to hear the words he knew his father was waiting to say: *You failed me, Todd.*

16

The landline phone at the Sorensen house had a cash box next to it. Calls cost a dollar. *Sorensen should start his own discount store*, Todd thought. Everything cost a dollar.

Todd found an old phone book propping up a bookcase and took it into his room.

"What's that?" Antonio asked. He laughed when Todd told him. He laughed at Todd a lot, at everything he said and did, at how he dressed, how he ate, even how he slept.

But soon Antonio and the other two boys left for school. Sorensen had kicked out another boy. Antonio said Sorensen liked to kick somebody out just to put fear into everyone else. Plus,

Antonio said, the more kids that cycled through The System, the more money Sorensen got from the county.

Meanwhile, Sorensen sat in the other room watching TV, as much as he wanted, unlike the one hour Todd was allowed. There wasn't anything he wanted to see anyway. All Todd wanted was to find his dad's lawyer. The name rattled somewhere in his mind; he'd know it when he saw it.

"You got that dollar?" Sorensen shouted at Todd from the other room.

Todd left the phone book open, went into the other room, and handed Sorensen the dollar. Sorensen muted the TV for a second. "Maybe you could spend it on some decent food," Todd said.

"Listen, Green River." Todd hated the nickname Sorensen had given him, which the other kids had adopted. "I get only so much money. You don't like the food, I can call and get you another placement. Pretty soon word gets around about you, and nobody in The System wants complainers. So, if I was you, unless you want to end up on the street, I'd shut my mouth."

Todd seethed inside, but said nothing. He went back into the kitchen and continued looking, going name by name, finally finding it. *Minneapolis has way too many lawyers*, he thought as he dialed the number. "Is Mr. Zukowski there?"

"Hold, please." After way too long, the same voice came on. "Who may I say is calling?" Todd explained who he was. Back on hold.

Every now and then, Todd set down the phone and peeked in at Sorensen. He was asleep at 3:30 in the afternoon.

More time passed, more bad music. Then, finally, "This is Ed Zukowski."

"Mr. Zukowski, this is Todd Morgan—"

"Todd, hold for a second."

The second turned into minutes until the lawyer came back on the phone. "I should've talked to you earlier, but I've been so busy." Todd glanced at the ad in the yellow pages. It seemed Zukowski did big business in personal injury suits and getting people off for DUIs.

"Why didn't my father make bail?" Todd asked. "When is he getting out?"

"Your father didn't have the financial resources," the lawyer replied. "And no friends or family to come forward to put up bail. You wouldn't happen to have a car?"

"I'm fifteen," Todd answered. "Dad owns a car."

"No, he leased a car," Zukowski said and coughed loudly. "I can't say much more."

"Dad says that you said I shouldn't talk to my sister. Is that right?" Todd asked. He imagined Zukowski sitting in a small office filled with overflowing ash trays.

"Well—" The lawyer was taking a while to come up with an answer. Maybe a response would cost a dollar.

"What's going on with my sister?" Todd pressed.

"Todd, here's the deal," Zukowski said. "It is imperative that you and your sister tell the same story. Understand?"

"But she—"

"That's all I can say about that. This is a very complicated situation with lots of moving parts. But there's one other thing your father wanted me to ask you."

"Yes?"

"How would you feel about skipping your mom's funeral?"

Todd felt like he'd been punched. First no one had told him about the funeral at all, and now . . . "Why? Why would he want me to do that?"

"If you show up, it won't look good for him. It'll look as if you're taking her side."

"But she's dead," Todd said. He meant it to be a flat, firm statement, but his voice wavered in a way he hated. His dad would've been ashamed. "It's not like they're still fighting over us. It's not like she can win."

"No, but your dad can still lose," said Zukowski. "In a big way."

Todd swallowed hard. His mom had never missed a meet. Wrestling, track, cross country, she'd been at everything. Cheering him on. Hugging him after each competition, before his dad stepped in for a high five or a stern lecture. Nothing had kept her away—not weather, not sickness, not arguments with Todd's dad. She'd always been there . . .

"OK, Mr. Zukowski," Todd said. "If it's what's best for Dad, I won't go." But his voice still wavered, no matter how hard he tried to steady it.

17

Peters was late, but Todd was ready. He had gotten a government ID card and they slipped in at the back of the line. As he came up the stairs, Todd saw the same old man with the cane outside.

"Will you be in there with me?" Todd asked. Peters nodded.

"Will you tell anybody what we talk about?"

A head shake this time. "Todd, you'll only have about twenty minutes," Peters said. They moved slowly up the line.

"Why such a short time?" Todd asked. Peters answered with a flurry of facts. It seemed every adult he'd met recently knew either too much or too little. Nobody was honest.

"ID, please," the guard said, and they finally made it to the front of the line.

"You the parent?" another guard asked Peters.

Todd laughed. The guard shot Todd a dirty look. He was good at it, Todd noticed. A real pro at hateful glares.

"No, I'm a guardian ad litem," she answered. "Here's all the paperwork."

The guard held the paperwork away like it was a foul-smelling thing. He set it in front of him, picked up the phone, said something Todd didn't catch, and then ordered the next person in line to come up.

"What's going on?" Todd asked Peters.

"I don't know," she answered. She tried to talk the guard, but he ignored her. They went back to the chairs. After ten minutes, half of the visiting time, a woman in a different-colored uniform came out. She stopped at the desk, conferred with the guard and read slowly through the paperwork. She motioned for Peters to speak with her, which ate up more time.

Finally, Peters motioned for Todd to join her. "Sorry that took so long, Todd."

Todd's fists clenched. "What was the problem?"

"The County is your legal guardian and if the judge says you can visit, you can visit," Peters said. "But that doesn't mean the people here will make it easy."

Todd looked up at the clock. It was 9:55.

It took him twice to clear the metal detector after forgetting to remove his belt. For a second, his mind flashed on the last time he'd gone through security at the airport, when his family took a trip together to Hawaii. It seemed like forever ago.

He started to run toward the visiting area, but a guard yelled at him to slow down. Another guard stood at the visiting area door. "No admittance fifteen minutes before—"

Behind him, Todd heard the first guard say, "It's OK, let him in."

"Which inmate?" the new guard asked. Todd told him. "He's been waiting for you."

Todd walked into a room that looked like a movie set. There was a wall with glass. On

Todd's side of the glass were people of all shapes and sizes, and on the other side were inmates, all of them clad in orange jumpsuits with numbers on the sleeves.

Todd grabbed the phone which connected his side to his father's. "Dad!"

"Junior, I'm glad you made it." His dad smiled, but his expression, like many Todd had seen over the past week, didn't look real. Nothing about this place seemed real. His father looked smaller, older, uglier, scarier. He was unshaven, with dark bags under his eyes.

"They listen in on these conversations so I can't say much," his dad said. "Now, you've always been my boy. You're a good son—I wish I could hug you, Junior. And I hope that soon you'll be able to hug your sister. Can you do that for me?"

"I'll do whatever you ask me to do."

"I *know* you will," his dad said, not comforting, but more like giving him an order.

"Like Mom's funeral. I didn't go because your lawyer said that you—"

His Dad cut him off. "You're a good son."

"Dad, why didn't you want me to go to Mom's—"

And again: "You're a good son."

Todd's father pressed his hand against the glass. Todd did the same, thinking of the high fives his dad gave him after wrestling wins. "I'll be out of here in no time, Junior. Just have some faith in me."

Todd didn't ask how his dad would get out of there if he couldn't make bail. He didn't ask why his dad didn't have money. He didn't ask anything else, period. He was too busy crying.

18

As Todd sat on the bus on the way back from the jail, he tried to imagine his mother's funeral last Saturday. Had he done the right thing, skipping it as his dad had asked? Not even asked, ordered. Todd had always followed his dad's orders. His mom hadn't . . .

He couldn't go back to Sorensen's. Not after everything that had happened today. He switched buses and headed to his own house instead.

The spare key still worked, although the alarm wasn't on. It didn't need to be, since there was little left to steal. The big-screen TV, the gaming systems, all of it was gone. Todd rushed into his room and found most of it intact, except for the TV, which also was missing. His computer was there, which seemed odd. His sister's room was more like the rest of the house: empty, totally empty. Not a piece of furniture, not a stitch of clothing; it was like Tina had never lived there.

Based on his limited experience, Todd doubted that any foster home would allow her to move in with all her belongings. She had to be somewhere else. In Iowa, probably, with their grandparents.

He had to find her. It was the only hope of getting his dad set free. He had to try again.

In the kitchen, Todd opened the fridge, one of the few remaining appliances. The light didn't come on. He flipped on a light switch. Nothing.

Looking around the dimly-lit kitchen, he realized he was standing where his mother's body had been. Someone had cleaned up the floor better than he had, but tiny specks of blood remained.

He replayed the scene once again in his

mind, but it was getting fuzzier. The yelling in the dining room, more yelling in the kitchen, then the knife. When Todd opened the drawer, he discovered the silverware was gone. His mom had pulled the knife, he knew that. He could picture it in her hand. But then, nothing.

He began opening other drawers until he found a small black book, his mom's address book. He rifled through the pages until he found the phone number for his dad's parents in Iowa. Todd lifted the receiver, but the phone was dead.

He started looking for the cash he knew his mom had hidden. His mom's things were mostly gone, but Todd found a twenty taped under the sink, and another twenty taped to the top of the fan. When he caught her hiding the money, Todd hadn't asked why she was doing it. But he guessed he'd be using it as she had intended—as getaway money.

***

At the Greyhound Bus station, he found several pay phones, but only one was working.

He dug out the change he'd gotten for one of the twenties at a nearby convenience store and opened the address book. First, he called Southeast High and pretended to be a family friend. He asked for Tina, but the school secretary wouldn't give him any information. Next he tried his grandparents' house in Iowa. No one picked up.

The bus ticket line was as long as any line he'd stood in lately. And that was saying something. Todd finally made his way to the front.

"I need a ticket to Des Moines—how much?" Todd asked the clerk.

"Depends, one way or round trip?"

Todd stumbled for an answer. His life used to be so easy—just do whatever his father told him. But now he wasn't sure that was best.

Todd heard voices behind him, grumbling from people who knew where they were going; people who knew their families, knew their homes. "Son, round trip or one way?"

Todd stared at the clerk and blinked the tears from his eyes. "One way."

19

Like the Minneapolis bus station, the one in Des Moines contained several pay phones. The first one he tried was in working order. Another call, another non-answer.

He'd gone all this way on faith. Now he'd go a little farther.

Outside the station, a few taxis waited. Todd climbed into one and handed the driver the address. The driver looked him up and down. "This is about a half-hour drive. You gonna be able to afford that?"

Todd's stomach clenched. How many bills did he have left? Probably not enough. He pulled out his wallet and started counting.

"Tell you what," said the driver. "I'll take you there, and you just pay me what you can."

Todd looked up in surprise. The driver was watching him with an expression Todd hadn't seen since his mom died. There was actual compassion in the man's eyes. Not the fake stuff Todd had gotten from the social workers and cops. *It must be pretty obvious that I'm in trouble*, Todd thought.

"Deal," he said. "Thanks."

The taxi left downtown and headed west into a setting sun. Eventually the driver pulled off the expressway and into a neighborhood of old houses. Memories from long ago rushed back, none of them good: loud arguments between his dad and his grandfather about nothing. Louder ones between his dad and uncles, doors slamming, tires squealing.

Todd handed the driver his remaining cash. As the taxi left, Todd knocked on the door of the house. He stared at the old Buick in the driveway. The door opened.

"Todd," his grandmother Pearl said. That was it, just his name. No surprise, no warmth, but no anger either. "Come in." She didn't hug or kiss him. There was no gushing about how he'd grown or anything else Todd might've assumed she'd say. Todd felt like a stranger in this house, just like he had at Sorensen's and Parker's places. Todd wanted to ask why they hadn't gotten in touch with him. But as he looked around the small living room and saw no photos of his father, he understood. They were on the other side. They were standing with Tina, against his dad, against their own flesh and blood.

"Is Tina here?" Todd asked.

His grandmother nodded. "I'll get her. Wait here for a minute." She motioned for him to take a seat in the small living room. When she left the room, Todd looked again at the photos all around him. There were school pictures of him and Tina taken throughout their childhood, but none of their parents. As if his grandparents had expected them to become orphans.

"Hi, Todd," Tina said from the end of the hallway. She kept her distance. Behind her, Grandpa Jim emerged, looking a lot older than the last time Todd saw him.

"We need to talk," Todd said to Tina.

"We've already talked," replied Tina. "And I told you. I'm not lying for Dad. Or for you."

"It was self-defense. You saw it!"

"You don't really believe that's what happened, do you, Todd?" Grandpa Jim asked quietly.

Todd stood up. "You weren't there! How would you know? How would—"

"I know my son," Jim said. "He uses people. Always has. And when they won't follow along with him anymore, he destroys them." Pearl nodded in agreement.

"He asked you not to call the police, remember?" Tina said. "And you agreed. You always said 'Yes, sir' and did what he wanted. Now he wants you lie for him, so he gets—"

"I know what I saw," Todd said, but as the words left his mouth, he felt doubt surface.

"No, I think you saw what he wanted you to see," Tina said.

Todd shook his head with all the force he had left. "He was trying to protect us!"

"No," said Tina again, her voice strangely steady. It was as if she'd finally run out of tears.

Todd was suddenly exhausted. He sank back down onto the couch. Tina came over and sat down next to him. Met his eyes. Was this the first time since that night that someone had looked him in the eye?

"He took the knife out of the drawer, Todd," said Tina. Quiet. Firm.

"*Mom* had the knife—"

"Mom grabbed it from him to keep it away from us, but then he grabbed it back. And he pushed her against the counter, and he hit her, like he always did, and then he stabbed her. He did it on purpose. Not in self-defense. He murdered her. He wasn't trying to protect us. And you don't have to protect him. You don't owe him anything."

"He's my father and I love him!" Todd shouted.

"Fear isn't love," Tina whispered. "You were afraid of him. So was I, so was Mom. He'd hurt us before. He was in control of all of us—until Mom tried to break away. That's why—"

"No!" Todd shouted, but his voice wouldn't hold steady.

Tina put a hand on his arm. "That's why he murdered our mother. You don't need to be afraid of him anymore. I'm not. You can say what you know is true."

Todd shut his eyes and replayed the scene again.

You won't take my kids from me, his dad had said.

The kitchen drawer opened, the knife removed and in his father's hand.

Todd tried to talk through his tears, but no questions came. Only answers.

20

Eight weeks later

Todd stood in line at the Hennepin County Jail for the last time. Tomorrow, his dad would be sentenced and sent to state prison. Mr. Zukowski had convinced him to plead guilty to third-degree murder, which meant a sentence of at least ten years.

Peters stood next to Todd. As Todd understood it, he was still a cog in The System. But at least he'd been allowed to stay in Iowa to live with his grandparents. They'd offered to drive him back to Minneapolis, but instead he'd taken the bus by himself again. Then he'd headed straight to the jail, deciding not to stop at Sorensen's for his belongings. There was nothing in his old life he needed, not even the photo of him and his father.

His new life was working out OK so far. He hadn't made the wrestling team—Iowa had serious wrestlers—but was doing OK in track. The school was nice, his grandparents nice enough, but most important, he and Tina were mending the hurt.

As he and Peters waited in line, Todd looked around. He recognized some of the faces, including the older man with the cane—late yet again, and being turned away, yet again. "I'm sorry this is such a mess," Peters said. "Your father isn't helping, with his custody request."

Todd nodded. "I guess he doesn't want to lose us . . ."

Peters stared at him. "I'm sorry no one told you," she said softly. "He's only fighting for custody of Tina."

Todd felt his knees buckle, but managed to maintain his wrestling balance. "What?"

"Your dad's willing to surrender his parental rights to you," Peters said. "Just not to Tina."

"Why would he do that?" Todd asked. His voice sounded far away, flat.

"He's not going to win," Peters said. "I think he just filed the claim for your sister as a symbolic gesture."

"To punish me for failing him," Todd heard himself say in that same dull voice. "For taking sides against him."

"You told the truth," Peters said. "You did the right thing."

"I took my mother's side," Todd murmured, more to himself than to Peters. "My family's side." For the first time in a long time, he allowed himself to think about his mom—who she was, how much she meant to him.

"Todd?" Peters called out. She was still standing in line, but Todd was walking away, past the back of the line, and then out the door.

Outside, Todd caught up with the old man with the cane. "Excuse me, sir. You want my place in line?"

A toothless smile filled the old man's face. "That's nice of you, son, but don't you have—"

"Don't worry about it." Todd put his hand on the man's back as they walked inside together. "I don't have any family in there."

AFTERWORD

As of 2014, it's estimated that more than 2.7 million children in the United States have a parent behind bars. About one in five of those kids are teenagers. While having parents in prison presents challenges at any age, it may be particularly hard for teenagers, as they try to find their way in the world.

The *Locked Out* series explores the realities of parental incarceration through the eyes of teens dealing with it. These stories are fictional, but the experiences that Patrick Jones writes about are daily life for many youths.

The characters deal with racism, stigma,

shame, sadness, confusion, and isolation—common struggles for children with parents in prison. Many teens are forced to move from their homes, schools, or communities as their families cope with their parents' incarcerations.

These extra challenges can affect teens with incarcerated parents in different ways. Kids often struggle in school—they are at increased risk for skipping school, feeling disconnected from classmates, and failing classes. They act out and test boundaries. And they're prone to taking risks, like using substances or engaging in other illegal activities.

In addition, studies have shown that youth who are involved in the juvenile justice system are far more likely than their peers to have a parent in the criminal justice system. In Minnesota, for example, boys in juvenile correctional facilities are ten times more likely than boys in public schools to have a parent currently incarcerated. This cycle of incarceration is likely caused by many factors. These include systemic differences in the distribution of wealth and resources, as well as bias within policies and practices.

The *Locked Out* series offers a glimpse into this complex world. While the books don't sugarcoat reality, each story offers a window of hope. The teen characters have a chance to thrive despite difficult circumstances. These books highlight the positive forces that make a difference in teens' lives: a loving, consistent caregiver; other supportive, trustworthy adults; meaningful connections at school; and participation in sports or other community programs. Indeed, these are the factors in teens' lives that mentoring programs around the country aim to strengthen, along with federal initiatives such as My Brother's Keeper, launched by President Obama.

This series serves as a reminder that just because a parent is locked up, it doesn't mean kids need to be locked out.

—Dr. Rebecca Shlafer
Department of Pediatrics,
University of Minnesota

AUTHOR ACKNOWLEDGMENTS

Thanks to Dr. Rebecca J. Shlafer and members of her research team for reading and commenting on this manuscript. Thanks to South St. Paul Community Learning Center, in particular John Egelkrout, Mindy Haukedahl, Kathleen Johnson, and Lisa Seppelt, for their continued support and collaboration.